Sleeping Beauty

STERLING CHILDREN'S BOOKS

New York

FROM A FAIRY TALE BY
Charles Perrault

TEXT ADAPTATION GIADA FRANCIA

GRAPHIC DESIGN MARINELLA DEBERNARDI

ILLUSTRATIONS BY

Francesca Rossi

Once upon a time, a king and queen ruled over a faraway land with kindness and generosity. For years they had dreamed of having a baby. All the people in the land were fond of the royal couple and prayed that their greatest desire would finally be fulfilled. But as much as they hoped and prayed, the royal couple's wish had never come true.

Doctors and wizards came from the four corners of the kingdom to try to help the king and queen. They each brought medicines and spells, but nothing seemed to work. One day, just when the couple's hope was beginning to fade, one of the fairies who lived in a great forest on the border of the kingdom appeared at the palace. She revealed to them a secret guarded for centuries by the inhabitants of the forest:

"There is a magical spring in the heart of the forest. Its water has extraordinary magical powers. Have some of it brought to the queen in a cask made of willow and use it for a long bath. What happens when you bathe in the water will surprise you!"

The king and queen followed the fairy's instructions. That night, they filled a bathtub with the magic water and the queen bathed in it. After a few minutes she was astonished to see a lobster appear in the bubbles!

"Your Majesty, do not be alarmed!" cried the creature. "As the fairy has already told you, these waters have incredible magical powers."

"But you . . . who are you?" asked the astonished queen.

"One of the spirits of the forest. I am here to tell you that we have heard your prayers and decided to answer them: you will have a daughter."

The king and queen were overjoyed. But nothing could match the joy they felt when the prophecy was fulfilled, and their daughter was born the following spring. They named her Aurora, after the goddess of the dawn, because she filled their lives with sunshine.

Everyone at the palace began preparations for a grand ceremony that would take place in honor of the baby. Nobility and rulers of neighboring kingdoms were invited to join the celebrations that would last a whole week.

The king gave orders for the castle to be decorated with flowers and fruit from the East. He ordered the curtains to be replaced with colorful hand-embroidered fabrics, and the garden to be decorated with long silk ribbons. The servants swept and polished every corner of the building and aired the one hundred guest rooms. A week before the ceremony, the cooks began to knead, chop, and roast. The maids polished the gold tableware reserved for the most important guests.

Hundreds of invitations were handwritten in gold ink by the palace scribe, and the fastest horsemen delivered them all across the land. But the king himself wrote the most important invitations: those for the woodland fairies, who had done so much to help him and the queen fulfill their greatest desire.

Although there were eight magical fairies of the forest, the king invited only seven. The eighth was the old fairy of the mountain. For decades she had been living alone in her cave, studying the dark arts, and no one remembered her anymore.

The long-awaited day of the ceremony finally came, along with the guests who began to arrive at the palace at the first light of dawn. The king and queen received every noble in the throne room, but when the chamberlain announced the arrival of the fairies, the royal pair went down to the main entrance with little Aurora in their arms to welcome them.

During the festivities, each guest went to little Aurora's cradle to present the wonderful gifts they had brought. The last to do this were the fairies of the forest, whose gifts were the most precious imaginable: seven spells that would secure for her the greatest virtues that anyone could wish for.

"Little Aurora, kindness will be yours," said the first fairy, waving her wand and letting a shower of golden sparkles fall gently on the baby's head.

"You'll be the bravest girl in the land," announced the second, hovering over the cradle.

"I give you generosity," whispered the third fairy, with a flick of her wand.

"We give you beauty and intelligence," chorused the fairy twins.

"You will be elegant and graceful; you will dance and sing like no other girl!" said the second-to-last, twirling her wand.

Then it was the youngest fairy's turn. She approached the cradle with her wand in her hand and raised it over her head. Just as she was about to give the gift of happiness, a gust of wind blew open the doors and a dense black smoke billowed into the room.

When the smoke finally cleared, the eighth fairy appeared in the center of the room. It was the old mountain fairy that no one had thought to invite.

"Is this the girl you did not want me to meet?" said the old fairy, pointing to little Aurora.

"This is our daughter," said the king. "But who are you?"

"She is one of our sisters, Your Majesty," said the first fairy. "She, too, protected the forest and its creatures. But then she turned her back on us to study the dark arts."

"And I have never regretted it, sister! I am a much more powerful sorceress than any of you will ever be, and I will not be ignored. It is a terrible insult!"

"I'm sorry if we have given any offense," said the king. "I hope you will forgive us."

"Yes, Your Majesty, but only if I can make a gift to the little princess myself," said the sorceress with an evil smile. Then she raised her stick, pointed it at the girl, and added:

"When she is sixteen years old, the princess will prick her finger on a spindle and die!"

The cruel fairy vanished in a black cloud, leaving the king and queen distraught and all the guests terrified.

"Fairies of the forest," the queen cried, "only you can save our child from this terrible fate!"

The youngest fairy, who had been interrupted by the witch's arrival, spoke up. "We cannot undo such an evil spell. But I still have my gift to give." She turned to the child. "Aurora, you will prick your finger on a spindle, but you will not die. You will fall into a deep sleep for one hundred years, from which you will be woken only by the kiss of true love."

The king nodded gratefully. That same evening, he issued a proclamation forbidding anyone in the kingdom to own spindles or needles. All spindles were brought to the palace and burned in the main courtyard.

"This should protect our daughter," said the queen as she stood before the great fire, holding her child.

Years passed without anything unusual happening.

As foretold by the fairies, the princess grew into a friendly and intelligent child. She was also very lively, as the governess who was entrusted with her care soon found out. And over the years, no governess ever managed to teach her how to behave like a traditional future queen. Aurora loved to escape her boring deportment lessons and go hide in the kitchen. She would sneak away from recitals to chase the birds in the palace gardens. She would even venture deep into the woods. There, she spent hours exploring trails, picking flowers, and chasing squirrels, only to return to the castle with her dress covered in mud, and pine needles in her long hair.

When the long winter days made it impossible to play in the gardens, Aurora explored the castle's endless rooms, followed by her struggling governess.

"If only one of your fairy godmothers had given you the gift of obedience!" the governess grumbled.

There was only one place on the palace grounds that Aurora had never explored: the old ruined tower.

For some reason, the tower held a great attraction for Aurora. Not even the princess could have said why she was so fascinated by this ancient building. But every time she passed it, she stopped to look at it. Curiously, there was no door or entrance to the tower—just an old stone staircase that spiraled around the wall.

Aurora was very brave, as foretold by one of her fairy godmothers. She had no fear of entering the tower, but she was too small to reach the stairs.

I could easily climb up there, but I have to grow up a little more, she thought to herself. *I have to grow until I'm up to that branch!*

Every spring, Aurora measured her height with a small notch in the bark of a nearby oak tree. Finally the day came when Aurora's head touched the branch. It was the year of her sixteenth birthday.

On that day, the palace was busily preparing a huge party for her. The king and queen woke their daughter with a hug and a bouquet of fresh flowers. They told her that they had to leave to spend the whole morning in the throne room attending to some guests, but then they would start the festivities together. After they left, Aurora gazed out her window. She could see the top of the old tower, and felt the irresistible desire to climb it.

While everyone was occupied with preparations for the party, she sneaked out of the castle and raced to the tower. She went up to the cracked and moss-covered walls, and put a foot on the first step. She looked up and saw with satisfaction that the second step was now easily accessible. She reached it with a leap and continued to climb until she was at the top of the staircase. There, she found a door.

"That's strange. I didn't know there was a room up here. I wonder what's in it?" she asked herself. The princess turned the doorknob and went in. The first thing she saw was an old woman spinning with a spindle.

"Oh, I didn't mean to disturb you," apologized Aurora. "I didn't think there was anyone here."

"Come here, my dear. I'm grateful for the company," replied the old woman, inviting her to come closer.

"What are you doing?" asked Aurora. "What is that?"

"It's a spindle, Your Highness. It's for weaving. Would you like to try?"

Aurora had never seen a spindle before. Curious, she went closer and reached out her hand. But in doing so she pricked her finger and a drop of blood appeared.

"Oh!" cried Aurora, dropping the spindle. "What's happening to me?"

Her head started to swim. Suddenly she felt weak and tired.

"Perhaps you need to sleep," chuckled the old woman. "And so my revenge is complete!"

The old weaver was in fact the old fairy of the mountain! She had returned after sixteen years to take her revenge on

the king and queen who had so deeply offended her.

"I . . . I cannot sleep now. They are waiting for me at the party . . . Everyone will be worried . . ." Aurora's voice trailed off as her eyes closed.

"Don't worry about that, girl. No one will be awake to notice your absence," said the witch.

Aurora drifted into a deep, enchanted sleep.

At the moment
the princess
fell asleep,
life in the castle
stopped as
well.

Suddenly, everyone in the palace fell asleep. In the kitchen, the cook fell to the ground in front of the fireplace, still holding a ladle in his hand. The fire that blazed in the fireplace burned down and the roast stopped sizzling. On the main staircase a servant, who was carefully carrying three bottles in his arms, slumped down on the steps, clutching the bottles to himself. A guard at the palace gates leaned against his spear and closed his eyes with a sigh. The nobles in the throne room smiled at one another and fell asleep, clasped in one another's arms. Even the king and queen were unable to suppress their yawns, and they fell asleep on their throne.

The animals were also affected by the witch's spell. The royal hounds lay down. The cats who had been intent on scrounging tasty morsels in the kitchen did the same. The horses waiting in the stables drowsed, and even the flies buzzing around them stopped moving.

The palace grounds were eerily quiet.

Every living thing became still and slept. And an unnatural silence, destined to last one hundred long years, reigned over the palace.

Soon, the courtyards and the paths were covered with moss and ivy. Around the castle grew a thick thorny hedge. Every year the hedge grew higher and higher, until it completely encircled and covered the castle. Eventually, nothing could be seen of the palace, not even the flags on the roof.

With the passing of the years, the legend of Sleeping Beauty, as the princess came to be called, spread far and wide. It told of a princess in a high tower waiting to be saved by a loving kiss. Attracted by the tales of her beauty and kindness, many knights came to the kingdom over the following decades, determined to get past the thorns in an attempt to reach the tower. But no one was able to make it. The thorns gripped them as if they were the claws of a beast, and the knights became entangled and died miserably.

One hundred years passed. Over time, people forgot about the castle hidden from sight. No more knights came, determined to break the spell. The legend of the beautiful sleeping princess became nothing more than a fairy tale to tell children at bedtime. One day, however, a prince arrived from a kingdom far, far away.

He had never heard of Sleeping Beauty, but he had undertaken the long journey for a hunting expedition. Without any companions other than his own horse, he had crossed the enchanted forest. But he had not been able to get beyond an ancient wall of thorns, behind which he had glimpsed the tops of old ruined towers. The prince went to the village that lay at the edge of the forest and entered the tavern. He ordered dinner and asked the innkeeper if he knew about the strange walls that could be seen between the trees.

"It's the court of the spirits," the innkeeper answered.

"Not at all," said a woman. "It's an ogre's castle! He lurks behind those walls to eat lost travelers that he surprises in the forest."

"Where'd you hear that?" asked the innkeeper, laughing.

"Everyone knows that! Only that monster is able to get through the sharp thorns."

The prince laughed. He was enjoying listening to these fanciful stories, when an old farmer sat down beside him and said: "I know what's behind the thorns. More than fifty years ago, my grandfather told me that a princess lived in that castle, and she was beautiful. She was placed under a spell that meant she would sleep for more than a century, until she was woken with a kiss of love from a brave man."

"A beautiful princess?" said the prince. "If the legend is true, then I must free her from the spell."

"Wait, young prince! Don't be too hasty. What I still have not told you is that many have tried before you. There were great warriors who braved the thorns with their weapons, and wizards who came from afar who tried to overcome them with potions and spells. Every single one failed, and every one paid with his life."

But now the prince could not help but think of Sleeping Beauty. That night he even saw her in his dreams.

At dawn, the young man left the village and rode up to the wall of thorns, unaware that this day was the hundredth anniversary of the spell. But when he reached the bush, beautiful flowers had replaced the thorns. The curse was fading.

As he reached the castle courtyard, the prince saw the horses and hunting dogs lying on the ground. On top of the walls, doves were sitting with their heads under their wings. It was so quiet that he could hear his own breathing.

Walking on the battlements, the young man came across guards and servants, huddled for decades in positions in which the spell had frozen them. He noticed that they all wore strange clothes and had hairstyles that had not been in fashion since before he was born. He saw two young men smiling in their sleep and holding one another as if about to make a somersault. The prince gazed about him in amazement when a thought struck him. He realized that he was seeing a reflection of a day of celebration interrupted a hundred years before. Enchanted by this thought, he went to the kitchen. There, he saw a cook stretching out his hand to grab the kitchen boy. The kitchen boy had been running away with a chicken that he was supposed to have plucked for a banquet being prepared a century before.

Advancing slowly, the prince arrived at the main hall. He saw nobles and their servants lying side by side, wrapped in the flags that they had once waved and flown with pride. At the far end, on the throne, the queen slept in the king's embrace.

The prince passed them all by and headed for the gardens, where he found himself at a high tower. He climbed the stairs two at a time and arrived at the top. He hesitated.

"Will I be able to break the spell?" the prince asked himself, as he gazed at the closed door. After a moment, he shook his head. "No more time-wasting! I made it as far as the threshold of her room, where no one has been before. This must be a sign."

He turned the handle firmly and opened the door to the room. Aurora was sleeping with a sweet smile on her lips. The prince approached her cautiously and looked for a long time at her serene and beautiful face, then reached out and gently stroked her hair. He was surprised to see that his hands were trembling. He smiled, feeling happy and excited at the same time.

It was time to find out if he was able to wake the sleeping beauty. The prince leaned over and kissed Aurora. The room lit up as if the sun had just risen on a new dawn.

The spell was broken!

When the beams of light reached the princess's face, her eyelashes fluttered. She slowly opened her eyes and yawned. Thus, Aurora woke from her deep sleep, and so did everyone throughout the palace. The cook began to chase the young boy; the servant brought to the table the three bottles that he had held in his arms for a hundred years; the flies resumed their flight, and the dogs barked excitedly.

In the throne room, the king and queen looked at each other in surprise. Then they realized that Aurora must have woken up and started looking for her and calling her name.

"I'm here!" said the princess, entering the room on the arm of a happy prince.

From that day, and for over a month, there was great feasting in the palace to celebrate the breaking of the curse and the marriage of Aurora, which was blessed by the spells of her sweet fairy godmothers.

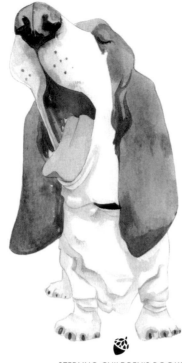

STERLING CHILDREN'S BOOKS
New York
An Imprint of Sterling Publishing
387 Park Avenue South
New York, NY 10016

STERLING CHILDREN'S BOOKS and the distinctive Sterling Children's Books logo are registered
trademarks of Sterling Publishing Co., Inc.

First Sterling edition 2015
First published in Italy in 2014 by De Agostini Libri S.p.A.

© 2014 De Agostini Libri S.p.A.

ISBN 978-1-4549-1512-6

Distributed in Canada by Sterling Publishing
c/o Canadian Manda Group, 165 Dufferin Street
Toronto, Ontario, Canada M6K 3H6
For information about custom editions, special sales, and premium and corporate purchases,
please contact Sterling Special Sales at 800-805-5489 or specialsales@sterlingpublishing.com.

Translation: Contextus s.r.l., Pavia, Italy (Louise Bostock)
Editor: Contextus s.r.l., Pavia, Italy (Martin Maguire)

Manufactured in China
Lot #:
2 4 6 8 10 9 7 5 3 1
11/14
www.sterlingpublishing.com/kids